Nicky

Davy   Donny   Daisy

Copyright © 1998 by Nord-Süd Verlag AG, Gossau Zürich, Switzerland.
First published in Switzerland under the title *Fröhliche Weihnachten, Pauli*.
English translation copyright © 1998 by North-South Books Inc.

First published in the United States, Great Britain, Canada,
Australia, and New Zealand in 1998 by North-South Books,
an imprint of Nord-Süd Verlag AG, Gossau Zürich, Switzerland.

Distributed in the United States by North-South Books Inc., New York.

Library of Congress Cataloging-in-Publication Data is available.
A CIP catalogue record for this book is available from The British Library.
ISBN 1-55858-980-5 (trade binding)
TB 10 9 8 7 6 5 4 3 2 1
ISBN 1-55858-981-3 (library binding)
LB 10 9 8 7 6 5 4 3 2 1
Printed in Belgium

For more information about our books, and the authors and artists
who create them, visit our web site: http://www.northsouth.com

Merry Christmas,
Davy!

Brigitte Weninger
Illustrated by Eve Tharlet

Translated by Rosemary Lanning

A MICHAEL NEUGEBAUER BOOK
NORTH-SOUTH BOOKS / NEW YORK / LONDON

Christmas was coming. The woods were buried under a thick blanket of snow, but the Rabbit family was safe and warm inside its burrow. Father Rabbit sat in his armchair and told the children all about Santa Claus.

"What does Santa Claus like us to do?" he asked them finally.

"He likes us to be good," said Davy.

"And to help one another," said Donny.

"And to share things!" added Daisy.

"And to be kind and loving," said big brother Dan.

"I see you have all been paying attention," said Father, smiling. "Now it's time for bed."

The next day Davy stayed indoors. He didn't want to go outside
because it was so cold. He sat by the window with Nicky, his toy
rabbit, waiting for the rest of the family to come home. Davy saw
a tiny bird hopping up and down, pecking the snow.
"Look, Nicky, he's trying to find something to eat," said Davy,
"but he won't find anything. The snow is much too deep.
Poor little bird."
Davy saw more birds nearby. Their feathers were fluffed up to
keep out the cold, and they all looked very hungry.

Davy remembered what Father had
said last night. "Santa Claus likes us to
help one another."
"I'll go and find some food for the birds,"
he said.
Davy ran into the larder and looked
around. He saw a big sack of corn. The
birds would like that. He lifted the heavy
sack down from the shelf and carried
it outside.

Where could he put the corn, he wondered, so
that it wouldn't get covered by snow?
The snow wasn't so deep under the old pine
tree, so Davy scattered the corn there.
"Now the birds will have enough to eat," he said.
As he carried the empty sack back into the
burrow, he saw the deer.

Davy thought of the other woodland animals.
The wild pigs' food lay buried under the snow, and the squirrels
were sure to have trouble finding their hidden stores.

Davy filled his little red hood
with apples, carrots, and acorns,
and ran over to the pine tree
once again.
"There!" Davy said to himself.
"Mother and Father will be so
pleased with me for helping
the animals. Santa Claus will
be happy too!" He could hardly
wait for his family to come home.

They soon returned to the burrow.

"Hello, Davy," said Mother. "Have you been good?"

Then she noticed that the larder door was open, and saw the half-empty shelves.

"Davy!" she cried. "Where has our food gone?"

"I...I...gave it to the hungry animals," Davy stammered.

"Are you crazy?" shouted Dan. "What are *we* going to eat all winter?"

Davy hadn't thought of that.

He turned to his father.

"You said we should help others, and share things, and love one another. We had so much, and the animals out there had nothing, so I..."

Davy's eyes filled with tears.

"Wa-a-a-a!" wailed Daisy. "Davy has given our food away. Now we're going to starve!"

"Dinah hungry!" squeaked their baby sister.

And Donny muttered, "What a fool!"

"Don't say that," said Father. "Davy meant well, and he is right. We had a lot, and the other animals had very little, so we shared our food. But don't worry, we won't go hungry."

"That's true," said Mother. "Things could be much worse. If we are careful, our food will last until spring. What's important is that we love and help each other now. Will you all promise to do that?"

"We will," they promised.

Time flew by until Christmas. Everyone was very careful not to waste any food. Sometimes Davy didn't even eat all of his share. He took the last few crumbs over to the pine tree and scattered them on the ground. He didn't want the animals to think he had forgotten them.

Then it was Christmas Eve. The rabbits were decorating their Christmas tree when they heard a loud knock on the door. Who could it be?

"Is it Santa Claus?" whispered Daisy.

Davy certainly hoped it was. He ran to the door.

But when he opened it, he saw birds, deer, squirrels, and wild pigs standing outside.

One of the birds chirped: "Davy, dear friend. We are so grateful to you for helping us, and we want to give you a Christmas present."

He held out a twig, laden with berries. "Next summer we birds will show you where the sweetest berries grow," he said, "and you can pick as many as you want."

One of the deer gave Davy a small bundle of wheat. "We deer will show you fields of beautiful wheat." The squirrels had brought some mushrooms. "We squirrels will show you where the biggest mushrooms grow," they said. And a wild pig dropped some carrots and an apple at Davy's feet. "We pigs know where to find the juiciest apples and fattest carrots," he grunted.

"Merry Christmas, Davy!"
cried all the animals. Then they
slipped quietly back into the woods.
"Look what my friends brought!"
Davy said to his family.

They carried the gifts indoors and laid them under
the Christmas tree.
"Mmm, these look delicious," said Davy.
Mother smiled. "Now I have enough apples and
berries to bake a Christmas cake," she said.
"Dinah hungry!" squeaked the baby.
Davy put a berry in her mouth.
"Try this, little Dinah," he said.
"Next summer you can have
lots more. My friends will
show us where all the
nicest things grow."

"And we will have so much food that we will share it with
the animals again. No one will be hungry next winter,"
said Mother.
Then they hugged each other and said, "Merry Christmas,
everyone! Merry Christmas, Davy!"